AN RMP BL

Awakening the Power of Self-Publishing

The Ultimate Guide

RUDO MUCHOKO

First published by RMPublishers Ltd 2022

Special thanks to RMPublishers Ltd. contributors and researchers.
Editors - Nonsikelelo Mkwananzi, Pao Viola Mbewe
Researchers: Uratile Nare, Tanatswa Chagonda, Sesethu Batala,
Cover Design: Badrudeen Mikaheel, Pao Viola Mbewe

First edition

ISBN: 978-1-7395928-8-2

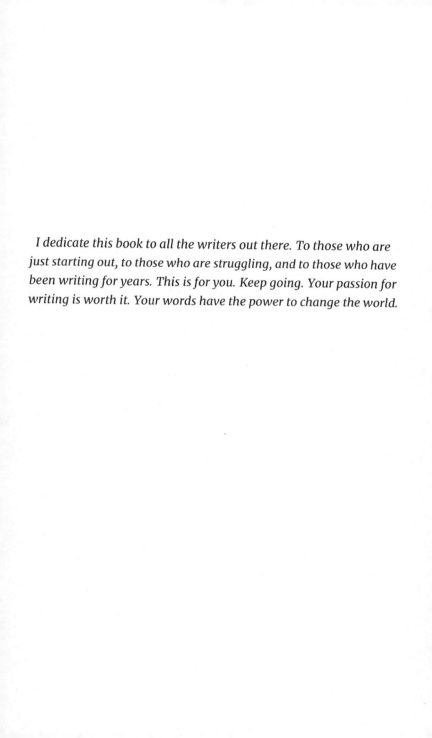

I dedicate this book to all the writers out there. To those who are just starting out, to those who are struggling, and to those who have been writing for years. This is for you. Keep going. Your passion for writing is worth it. Your words have the power to change the world.

Contents

Foreword

Tunji Olujimi - Book Publishing Coach|Speaker| Author|Pastor

The world is waiting on you to share your message, your story, and your content. There is something in you that needs to come out on display through your words. Now is the time to awaken that giant within you; now is the time to get that book written; and now is the time to publish your message.

When it comes to writing and publishing a book, people often only think of Penguin Random House, HarperCollins, Hachette Book Group, Simon & Schuster, and other household names in the traditional publishing space. But there is another way that people don't really explore. This book gives you everything you need to know about the new way of publishing. Why is reading this book so refreshing? Because most authors don't give you details. *Awakening the Power of Self-Publishing* is a book that doesn't hold back on the information the author needs to really become successful in the self-publishing industry.

Self-publishing is the new way to become a successful author in this day and age. It makes sense to take a leap of faith and try it out. You can't go wrong if you do it the right way.

Becoming an author is the fastest way to credibility, authority, and profitability, and that's why using the self-publishing method is the easiest way to get you there fast. There are no more gatekeepers who ask you for all the information in the world and need to know if you are famous or have a following before they can give you a contract. With this new method, you are able to share your content, story, and message with the world in less time and still have an effective launch.

With self-publishing, you can make a more significant impact, have much more influence, and increase your income as a self-published author. You can build your profile and also build your business, which most people can't do with traditional publishing. You have so much more room to manoeuvre in this new space.

Anyone who reads this book has the right tools to go from having no idea to being a published author in no time because the author has laid out everything the aspiring author is looking for when thinking of becoming an author. You can literally go from idea to author with the information in this book.

Rudo has done a great job explaining to the reader, step by step, what is needed in the process of self-publishing. I really like her style of writing and how easy the book is to read and understand. You can't go wrong if you implement the methods taught in this book.

Let the sleeping giant in you awaken now to the power of self-publishing and do what's needed to get your book written in 2023 and get it published so you can become that published author you've always dreamed of becoming. Now is the time to start awakening to the power of self-publishing!

Preface

There's no definitive answer to the question, "How do I get published?" After all, every author's journey is unique. But some tried-and-true tips can help you along the way. My personal self-publishing journey wasn't without a glitch, and this inspired me to learn the process for myself. Once I discovered I was interested in publishing books, I decided to enrol in a Publishing and English course at University.

If you're looking for guidance on getting started in publishing, or support as you navigate the publishing process, then this book is for you. This book contains the advice you need to make your ambition of becoming a best-selling author a reality, regardless of where you are in your publishing career or how far along you are.

I started RMPublishers Ltd to help first-time authors become published. The company has been on a digitisation journey, creating publications, audiobooks, podcasts, and most recently, a virtual book store. Digitisation allows us to move towards digital formats accessible to anyone, anywhere. We are constantly innovating and expanding our product range to meet the evolving needs of our customers.

I remember, before social media was what it is now, I joined a

Yahoo group for fiction novels called *LiveLoveLaughandBooks*. It was such a delight to hear from the authors whose books I had read. It made me feel connected to them, although I had never met them in person. Being young at the time, I had limited resources, and since they were based mostly in America, I always wished I could join them at their book events. The African-American authors seemed to have book events every weekend. Somebody was launching a new book somehow, and it seemed to be so much fun, based on the post-event pictures and reports. If they didn't have a group like this, they may not have been able to reach millions worldwide. Sadly, this group closed down, and one of my favourite authors, Katherine Jenkins (RIP), sadly passed on, but this group was the reason I frequented the library. In the days before WiFi, the library was my favourite place to access computers and borrow books. This piqued my interest in writing and, subsequently, in publishing.

Being an author is an incredible accomplishment. The self-publishing process might be difficult, but with perseverance, hard work, and dedication, you can effectively establish your author brand. Finding a publisher who can assist you in turning your manuscript into a book is possible once you determine why you are writing it. To get your book noticed, you need a solid marketing strategy. Once you become a published author, however, it's not time to kick back; instead, you must continue to market your book and find ways to make money from it. You will be assisted and led through the self-publishing process by the advice in this book. I hope your adventure is successful!

Acknowledgement

I would like to thank the researchers and writers who have contributed to this company book. Thank you for helping me research and develop this project. Thank you to Pastor Tunji Olujimi for taking the time to write the foreword for this book. Thank you also to RMPublishers Ltd for giving me the opportunity to publish my work.

1

Becoming an Author

Everyone dreams of becoming an author, especially in today's digital age where people have access to many platforms to make their authorship dreams come true. Becoming a successful author takes a lot of hard work, dedication, and determination. Some people become discouraged when they see other authors' and their books' sales skyrocket and even achieve best-seller status. The short of it is that you need to have a great marketing plan for your book even to gain traction. For most authors, the dream starts and ends with Amazon. The sad news is that without promotions, an online presence, and a marketing plan in place, your book is just going to disappear into the abyss of Amazon products, as these update daily and are constantly evolving.

The following will help you understand why it doesn't take overnight to become a successful best-selling Amazon author:

1. Most people expect to see their book at the top of Amazon's best-seller list without putting in much effort. This is

simply not the case. You might not see success immediately on Amazon. It can take several months for your book to gain traction and sell copies. After it does, it will probably climb up the best-seller lists slowly. During this time, you'll need to focus on writing quality content for your book and promoting it effectively through social media channels like Facebook and Twitter.

2. Amazon's algorithm works differently from other search engines like Google Search or Apple. You won't be able to directly target potential readers with ads on your book's pages or in its app store like you can with Google AdWords or Facebook Ads. Instead, you'll need to find other ways to reach potential readers— for example through forums and social media pages.

3. Many successful Amazon authors enjoy the fact that they've worked hard to achieve their status. They know that no one ever became a bestselling author overnight and considering this helps them stay focused on their goal instead of getting discouraged easily by slow progress. They know that slow progress is necessary for fast success since it allows them to spend time improving their strategies for gaining traction with their books, instead of becoming impatient and abandoning their work altogether after a few slow months of slow sales without making any real progress whatsoever towards their goal at all.

4. Becoming an Amazon bestselling author isn't easy, but anyone willing to put in the time and effort can achieve this goal if they are willing to persevere long enough for slow success rather than instant success on this platform. While there are certainly some who achieve instant success with minimal effort, doing so leads away from the path most

will find most conducive towards achieving real success as an Amazon bestselling author in the long run.

So, how do you turn this around?

There's no doubt that building an audience for your work is necessary for making a living as an author. Readers are essential for any writing business; without them, no books would ever be published. However, many aspiring authors struggle to attract attention to their work unless they can find ways of marketing their writing talents to potential readers first. Social media platforms such as Facebook and Instagram allow authors to connect with potential readers and build their base rapidly. Influencers and brands can also help to promote the works of authors, giving them greater exposure and earnings. Using different marketing techniques can speed up the process of building your audience. This is expanded more in the marketing chapter. You can also ask family and friends to spread the word about your book.

Best Seller Status

Ever heard of "best-seller" status? Isn't it lucrative to become one? Imagine your name bearing the Best Selling Author title—can you see it? After your book has been published, you will want to get the marketing right. However, marketing starts way before you even write the book. It is important to get the buzz going.

Well, the likes of New York Times bestsellers, Amazon best sellers, etc. are not going to happen overnight and without a plan. And most of these best-selling lists are reflective of books selling well in bookstores and online retailers and have nothing to do with the contents. Uploading your book for sale on Amazon is not enough. There are a few things you can try to achieve best-seller status:

Write a great book

This seems obvious, but it's the most important thing for you to do. Write something that people will want to read—a well-crafted and engaging book.

Get the buzz going

Try to generate interest in your book before it is released. Create a website or blog dedicated to your book, and start promoting it. Get people talking about it on social media, and try to get reviews in advance from well-known reviewers or bloggers.

Create a good marketing plan

Once your book is out, make sure you have a good strategy for getting it in front of potential readers. This might include doing some publicity yourself or working with a publicist. Implement creative marketing techniques such as book trailers or social media campaigns.

Get your book into the right hands

Make sure potential readers, who will both enjoy and recommend it, are aware of it. This might mean sending out review copies, giving talks or readings at bookstores, or participating in online discussion forums about books in your genre.

Be patient

Bestseller status doesn't happen overnight. It takes time, hard work, and a little bit of luck. But if you keep at it, you just might find yourself on the bestseller list one day.

2

An Author as a Brand

A uthor credibility is essential when viewing yourself as a business or brand because it highlights that you are reputable and trustworthy to the outside world. When determining the credibility of an author, one can consider the following:

- Professional Affiliations
- Academic and professional credentials
- Reputation
- Prior publications

These are the stepping stones that will determine your qualifications for the topics on which you are writing. Are you working in the field in which you are writing? Are you associated with equally credible people? These are the questions that both professionals and non-professionals consider before determining their credibility.

Establishing an author brand can be confusing, tedious, and

sometimes painful. On the other hand, starting a book business is a profitable business idea. Retail book sales exceed US$16 billion per year in the USA alone, and authors can tap into this lucrative market.

The most important marketing weapon for your book is yourself. Customers and prospects will look to you first to provide the answers they need to solve their problems because your book proves that you have the expertise required to make that happen. A book can sell well even if it never makes the bestseller lists. But, by publishing a book that is uniquely positioned, well-targeted, content-rich, well-written, well-designed, and assiduously promoted, it will establish a level of thought leadership that leaves other competitors in the dust.

While starting an author's journey can be a lot of work, becoming self-published offers a variety of advantages. For example, in a self-publishing company, there is creative control over your book, unlike with traditional publishers. While you can self-publish a book entirely on your own (including formatting and uploading) or go through a self-publishing publisher, many readers and bookstores have a bias against self-published books, although this is changing significantly. They think the books haven't gone through a rigorous selection or editing process. However, listing a publishing company in the book's details will make readers and bookstores more likely to pick up the book. Many self-published books have gained the media's attention, and several have been or are being turned into films.

Building your author brand requires interaction with your readers. This means having a social connection with your readers, be it online, through event gatherings, or by going to places that they frequent. Once you've written your work, you want to find ways to stay relevant, and I have the checklist in the preceding chapters for you.

3

The Book Writing process

You can get your book in a variety of formats, ranging from a word file to a fully tangible book. First, you ought to have written material. Have content and establish that the content is plagiarism-free. Ever heard the saying, "If you're looking for a book that's not on the shelves, write it yourself?" That notion rings true! It's imperative to think about **the content** that you would like to share. Even if you use other sources to support your points, you ought to reference them and give credit.

Having worked with several self-help titles and Christian books, it's imperative for authors to highlight where they get their scriptures from. There is a free version of the Bible that you can use, but there's also a fair usage policy. It is not necessary to copy half a chapter of a Bible verse to propel a pony forward. Enable your readers to be proactive by suggesting they complete reading the chapter from their own Bible. And sometimes people don't always have the time, but it's necessary to keep things short and to the point.

Questions to ask yourself:

- Is there a market for your book? – Do thorough market research
- Does your book offer valuable or useful information?
- Who in the niche/market has written similar work? Is it selling?
- How can yours be different?

You cannot expect someone else to write about the topics that you feel passionate about. In essence, you have to get up, do the needful, and put in some work. Writing is different for many people. Some find it easy; for others, it's a chore, and some struggle through the process, especially when hit by writer's block. The idea is to just write! It will make sense once you start the editing process by moving chapters around. But to get started, you must write something down.

Ghostwriters

For those authors who require assistance, a ghostwriter can be hired. This will enable you to communicate your ideas with them, and they'll write the book for you. As it is a paid service, make sure you understand the terms of the agreement and have an interest in getting involved at every stage. Again, if the communication is not effective, the ghostwriter cannot articulate what you are trying to say. You will need to read the work and read it again until you're satisfied with what your book communicates to the world.

Editors

After establishing the written content, the next step is to find an editor to help with structure, editing, and proofreading. It is a good idea to invest in an editor and proofreader because they help you with grammar and punctuation as well as sentence construction to avoid your sentences looking cannibalistic, for example:

"Let's eat, Grandma vs. Let's eat Grandma."

Normal: Let's eat, Grandma.

Cannibalistic: "Let's eat Grandma."

Editors and proofreaders come in different shapes and forms; do your research and find the one that best suits you. Editors and proofreaders don't come cheap either, so make sure you budget wisely for that. Some publishers have editing and proofreading in-house, like here at RMPublishers, where our packages come with editing and proofreading as standard. This makes life much easier for an author who is just starting out on their writing journey.

What if I edit my own work?

A frequently asked question! This works if you're confident in your editing skills; however, it doesn't hurt to let a professional do the work for you, after all, it is their area of expertise. When I first published my fictional book, *When Love Strikes*, I had limited knowledge about the publishing process. I remember being excited about the prospect of my printed paper files turning into a book that I didn't do due diligence on. It took people criticising my work for me to "wake up." Harsh critics are important for the benefit of our improvement. So next time when someone gives you a "harsh comment," remember to take it as constructive criticism and move on.

After editing and proofreading, we come to design. You want your book to have the best possible chance of selling. The book cover design chapter elaborates more on this.

Book Formatting

When formatting your book's interior, there are a few key things to keep in mind. First and foremost, you want to make sure that the design of your book is clean and easy to read. This means choosing an appropriate font size and style and making sure that there is adequate white space on the page. Additionally, you'll want to pay attention to small details like chapter headings and page numbers.

Another important aspect of book interior formatting is the layout of the pages. These need to be consistent throughout the entire book. This includes things like margins, indentations, and spacing between lines of text. By taking care to maintain a consistent layout, you'll give your book a professional look that will help it stand out from the competition.

Finally, make sure your book is properly paginated. This means each page starts and ends at the correct place, and there are no blank pages or extra pages within the book. Proper pagination is essential for creating a professional-looking interior.

By taking care of your book's interior formatting, you ensure that it looks its best and stands out from the competition. With a little attention to detail, you can create a book that is easy on the eyes and a pleasure to read.

4

The Editor's Role

Writing a book is an exciting endeavour, but it is also a tedious one. Anyone who completes a manuscript deserves a professional editor. An unedited manuscript is a mess and can never meet the expectations of its readers. It often contains grammatical errors, awkward sentences, and weak ideas. Apart from making your work difficult to read, this state also makes it difficult to publish.

In addition to improving the flow of writing, an editor helps craft your message for the reader's benefit. In the past, publishing companies would not accept manuscripts unless they were edited first. To make sure that they accept your work, you should get an editor to polish your manuscript before sending it off. Plus, having an editor makes your work easier by fixing punctuation and grammatical errors.

A professional editor knows how to improve your manuscript. As such, they will look for weak ideas and refine what's left into a strong argument. They will also look for grammatical errors and fix these as well. By investing in an editor, you ensure that your work meets the standards of publication and improves as you go along.

Apart from making your work easier to read and edit, an editor can also help you improve the quality of your writing. Most editors are trained in different genres and can offer expert advice on how to write for this genre specifically. For example, if you are writing about sports, an editor can help you identify key terms that readers will easily understand. Your editor can then suggest appropriate words based on what they know about your topic as well as the type of audience you are targeting.

Investing in an editor is never regretted once you see the results! An edited manuscript is much easier to understand compared to an unedited version— both while reading and when being submitted for publication. Plus, having someone edit your work frees up your time so that you can focus on other aspects of writing books such as book proposals or book chapters/articles/reviews etc.

The stages of editing

A manuscript must be edited to meet the standards of the publisher and the reader. Every aspect of a book must be well-produced before it's accepted by a publisher. Many publishing houses have strict rules about the format, style, and layout of a book's pages. Each chapter must have its own font, size, and style so that it looks professional when combined into a book. Some books need more work than others since some publishers want lower-quality books than others do. Once an editor has finished with a manuscript, it will have been edited to meet all necessary standards.

A book goes through the following processes of development:

- Beta Readers
- Copy editing
- Story editing
- Self Editing
- Professional Editing
- Proofing

Beta readers

Beta readers are people who read your book in its early stages and provide feedback on its content, structure, and overall quality. This feedback can be invaluable in helping you improve your book before it is published. If you are thinking about publishing your book electronically, then you may be wondering whether or not you need to use beta readers.

Copy Editing

Copy editing is the process of reviewing and correcting errors in a text before it is published. This includes ensuring that the text is well-written, accurate, and free of any errors. Copy editors also pay attention to the overall flow and structure of the text, and they may make suggestions on how to improve it. Copy editing is an important step in the publication process, and it can help to make sure that your text is error-free and ready for publication. If you are planning to publish a text, whether it is an article, a book, or something else, you should consider hiring a copy editor to review it before it goes to print.

Story editing, professional editing, and proofreading are all important aspects of the editorial process. A book must be properly edited for the reader to get the full message. This is especially true if future readers want to learn from or apply what is stated in the text. Readers need clarity on what they should do after reading a how-to guide or motivational book—especially if they intend to act on its contents! An editor has several functions when editing books, but making sure that readers understand what they read is always important.

5

Book Cover Design

A lot of graphic designers are not **Book** designers. It is important to affiliate with a graphic design company or service that understands the needs and requirements of the publishing platform you choose. Book design transcends just the front and back covers. A designer who understands this concept can help shape your book in a way that will drive sales, that attract your book to readers and bookstores.

Book Cover Design Tips that Sell

The saying goes, "You can't judge a book by its cover," but there is no denying the importance of a visually impactful cover design. No matter how much time and attention is devoted to the interior parts, the cover plays a powerful marketing role.

Some questions to have when you are looking for cover design ideas are:

· Should your cover design be bold and dramatic?

- Should it be crisp and clean?
- Does the font choice matter?
- What book cover size should you use?

These and many more design elements are critical when deciding on the aesthetic container of your literary masterpiece!

So What Makes a Good Book Cover?

Our initial attraction to a book is likely due to its compelling cover design which then entices us to check out the "Look Inside" excerpts on the digital marketplace. In a brick-and-mortar bookstore, a book cover initially enables you to pick up the book and read the excerpt on the back.

A book cover design should:

- Communicate the theme, genre, and tone of the book.
- Evoke emotion or reaction.
- Be visually balanced.
- Be understandable.
- Be appropriate to the genre.
- Be visually appealing even as a thumbnail.

Front Cover Design Tips

Designing a beautiful book cover equals parts creativity and adherence to design standards. When these two elements come together in perfect harmony, the result is a cover that will attract attention and increase sales volume. To achieve this lofty goal, there are some critical steps to take. To design a good book cover, you must:

- Determine what you want the cover to convey and what story it tells.
- Decide on a colour palette.
- Create an attention-grabbing image or visual focal point.
- Select two compatible fonts to convey the title, subtitle, and author. Specific genes are associated with particular fonts.

Back Cover Design Tips

Consider the back cover a promotional device, offering essential details about the content and author and featuring reviews or awards received. Even though the back cover focuses on text, design is still essential. The visuals featured on the cover will wrap around the back cover. Consider these tips for your back book cover design:

- Write a compelling blurb about your book. This is equivalent to the ten-second elevator pitch that piques interest and inspires the person to buy the book to learn more. The blurb should be appropriate for its genre, such as asking questions and imparting information for non-fiction or giving an intriguing hint at the plot for fiction.
- Write a compact author bio. Keep it short and sweet.
- Include testimonials. Include two or three short blurbs if you have secured some reviews from a fellow author or someone in a prominent position in your chosen field. Be sure to emphasize the credentials of the person who wrote it.

The design should reflect the audience, such as the gender and age of the reader. An informative and concise subtitle is essential to defining the book's theme.

Communicate your ideas

Everyone perceives information differently. Be sure to use effective communication skills when you pitch your ideas to a designer. The picture you may have in your mind is not necessarily how the other person can articulate it on paper if you don't communicate clearly. Find examples to elaborate on your idea, send samples, and check with the designer if they understand the concept. If possible, get a draft first and shape the ideas together. Don't wait for a surprise cover. It's your work; you need to be actively involved at every stage. At the consultation stage, check that what you require can be executed before signing a contract. If you are looking for sophisticated designs, be prepared to pay for them.

Work With the Experts to Create the Perfect Book Cover

Coming up with a compelling book cover design can be one of the more challenging steps in self-publishing. A publishing team that can assist you in designing the book cover's trim size, selecting the font and colour palette, the overall visual theme and composition, and guidance on the back cover content. Different publishing platforms require different sizes so check the correct siding for your publication. Some printers also offer different printing trim sizes to that of digital printing platforms such as Amazon.

6

Self-publishing vs Traditional Publishing

Publishing is an industry that has grown exponentially in the last hundred years. In the early days of publishing, only major publishers could produce books. These publishing houses had access to expensive printing technology that made producing books a simple task. This was revolutionary for the masses, who could now read and learn.

A traditional book or publishing company is a business that creates and distributes copies of written work, which can be anything from children's books to novels, cookbooks, magazines, etc. Large publishing companies publish thousands of books a year under different "imprints," or departments. Publishing with a personal company grants an individual full control of their work.

Many self-published authors face a steep learning curve when it comes to their craft. Most traditional publishers aren't willing to take on new writers and may not even accept your manuscript. Self-publishing allows independent authors to produce and sell their work without interference from a traditional publisher. It also allows authors to retain copyright over their work, which can increase their earnings.

One cannot rely completely on anyone else to make their book a success unless, of course, you've been paid upfront for it, but even then, some mainstream publishers do not offer promotions for your book.

Self-publishing offers a number of advantages to both the author and the publisher. The author retains full creative control over his work and can publish when desired—or not publish at all. This gives authors more time for their writing and doesn't rush them into publishing if they aren't ready. Publishers can also focus on marketing their work instead of spending time formatting, uploading, etc. The author also pays no commissions or other fees to his publisher since self-publishing eliminates these costs altogether. Many self-published authors have found success with this model since it allows them to publish without first consulting a traditional publisher. A few traditional publishers are willing to take on new writers, but there aren't many compared to traditional publishers.

There are several benefits to self-publishing your work instead of waiting for a traditional publisher or waiting until you're ready for publication-quality control alone isn't enough reason in itself; it must be done well enough for you as an author to make money from it in the long run. While there are disadvantages, self-publishing is an excellent way for both independent authors and small publishers alike.

Self-publishing Platforms

There are several different self-publishing platforms to choose from, and the one that's right for you will depend on your specific needs, goals, and budget too! The cost of self-publishing can vary significantly depending on what service you use. Below are some of the different options available that can help you decide which one is right for you:

1. Kindle Direct Publishing (KDP) Owned by Amazon – KDP publishes and retails books that can be read on Kindle devices or on devices that have installed the Kindle app...
2. iBooks
3. Barnes & Noble Press
4. Kobo
5. IngramSpark
6. Smashwords
7. Draft2Digital
8. Lulu
9. Book Baby
10. Independent Publishers

The power of the ISBN

Self-published authors need an ISBN, a unique identifier for books. These are used to track book records and help with distribution. ISBNs are made up of 10 or 13 digits. The ISBN system was developed by the International Organization for Standardization (ISO) to make it easier to identify and track books. You can get an ISBN for your book through several different companies, including ISBN agencies Nielsen or Bowker.

When you create a record for your book on Nielsen, for example, you will need to include the ISBN to ensure that your book can be properly identified and tracked. You can register with a distributor who will enable your books to be sent to a store such as Waterstones and other online retailers.

Barcodes

Most self-publishing platforms and printers will provide a barcode for you. However, there are several retailers that can sell barcodes, including Nielsen. Find out what's best for your budget, but also inquire with your chosen publishing platform if they provide barcodes.

Book Distribution channels

In the olden days, books were distributed in libraries and bookshops. However, with the advent of printing, the printing press and later radio and television, the number of distribution channels increased. Today, books are distributed via many different media such as television, radio, internet, newspapers and more. Additionally, book distributors are also referred to as wholesalers or retailers.

Consumers now are able to get a copy of the book from any distribution channel they choose— whether it's from their local library or an online bookstore. On top of that, consumers no longer need access to bookshops where they can purchase their favourite titles; they can get their books delivered directly to their doorstep via internet retailers such as Amazon Prime or Book Depository.

There are several internet retail giants that sell books; however, some e-commerce platforms specialize in selling books instead. Other distributors include large retail chains have large catalogues containing thousands of titles from various publishers worldwide. In the UK, there are several book distributors the largest being Gardner Books and Baker & Taylor. Online distributors include Ingram Content Group. In the UK, you will need your book to be listed with Nielsen Book Data to have a record of your book and enable the distribution process, including the book depository.

Book depository

The biggest UK depository is the British Library. However, other libraries can help you. It's important to make sure your book is properly distributed, and one way to do that is through a legal deposit. A legal deposit is the process of depositing copies of your book in designated libraries. This ensures that your work will be available for future generations, and also helps with the marketing of your book.

There are a few things to keep in mind when considering a legal deposit:

1. Make sure that your book meets the requirements of the deposit.
2. Find a library that participates in the program.
3. Fill out the necessary paperwork.

Most Publishers handle this process for you so you only need to ask upon signing up what their process is.

7

Book reviews

What is a book Review?

A book review, simply put, is a critical evaluation of your book that is written by someone who has read it. Book reviews provide insight into what the book is about, and this is important as readers rely on them to decide whether to buy a book or not.

Reviews are not just about defining and describing your book, but also about providing an opinion on it; they are a form of feedback that readers offer to help other people make a decision about the book they are considering buying. They can be subjective or objective, and they can be positive or negative. Book reviews can have a significant impact on a book's sales because most readers rely on reviews to make purchasing decisions. Low reviews can have a negative impact on sales, although this is not always the case. A few other things can impact low book sales such as

1. The cover design
2. Genre
3. Author's reputation
4. Titles

Book reviews are different from a testimonial, which is a personal endorsement of your book! Testimonials differ from reviews because they do not provide opinions on the book's subject matter. Reviews can be positive, negative, or neutral in nature. However, most reviews are honest and unbiased in nature.

Key Benefits of Reviews for Authors

1. Boost or Build your Author Credibility - A well-written book review will entice a curious reader to read your book. Readers quickly get the gist of the book, themes, genre and storyline from a review and these are deciding factors that will make the reader decide whether or not to read or buy your book.
2. Feedback from readers helps the author improve their writing - It is crucial to gather reviews before your book is published so you can get important feedback helpful in improving your book and sales trajectory. If your book has already been published you can still gather reviews to help you improve your future writing. Once you get feedback from your readers, you can be sure to make your next book into a best seller.
3. Good reviews can lead to a positive impact on sales and ratings for your book on different platforms such as Amazon, Good reads, online retail stores and independent

bookstores.

4. Gather reviews from different platforms to get your book in front of thousands of readers which can have a positive outcome for your book and readership.

The influence reviews have on readers

People rely heavily on book reviews when deciding whether to purchase a book. This phenomenon has led authors to pay people to write good reviews about their books. This is a fairly popular concept since businesses and authors alike understand the influence reviews have on readers.

Here's a quick analysis of why some books get more reviews than others:

Using two books Frieda McFadden's *Locked Door* and Rob Peguero's *With Prejudice* a few details come to play;

1. The cover design – colour, fonts etc
2. Genre
3. Author's reputation – One is a New York Bestseller compared to the other one
4. Title descriptions – one is more thrilling than the other
5. The marketing strategies – budgets can play a role in audience reach depending on the author–publisher relationship.

Identifying the appropriate **genre** plays an important role in the success of your book. One of the factors that contributed to *The Locked Door's* success is its intriguing synopsis. A synopsis is a summary of a book, and Frieda McFadden provided an overview that piqued readers' curiosity. Rob Peguero's synopsis did not leave the reader wanting more. It gave way too much information, leaving the reader with little desire to know more. A synopsis needs to be precise and intriguing; this will make readers want to buy the book.

A **book cover's design** also plays a factor in getting great reviews. When writing in a certain genre, there are certain elements, such as colour and design, that are associated with that genre. The Locked Door's cover design has dark hues, such as black, that reflect the mystery genre. The use of the image of the door in the book design displays the thriller genre that the book is written in. Prejudice's book cover design, on the other hand, lacks the elements that are associated with the thriller genre. The cover design does not give a hint that the book is a thriller. The cover design, colours and fonts do not necessarily reflect that the book is a thriller.

An **author's reputation** plays a part in a book's success. A well-known author has already succeeded in fulfilling their audiences' expectations, which makes readers willing to buy the book. Frieda McFadden is Amazon's number one best-selling author thanks to her reputation. Readers trust her expertise as a physician, which she uses in her novels to deliver wonderful, thriller stories. As the number one best-selling author, McFadden's novels gain a lot of traction compared to Rob Peguero's *With Prejudice.*

Book reviews are influential as they make the book popular, reaching different audiences and communities. The last important factor in your book's success is cost. Costs can make a huge difference when it comes to purchasing a book. A higher-priced book can discourage a reader from buying it, especially if that book has low reviews, Rob Peguero's *With Prejudice* is an example. Peguero's novel has bad reviews because readers may have found out the book is not worth the money they spent. The accessibility of the book is a determining factor that measures its worth.

As you build your author credibility, make sure your reviews stand out to help your book become a success.

Where to get book reviews

While there are many places and many ways to get reviews, here are some recommendations:

1. Asking your friends, family and colleagues for a review.
2. The Book Network – https://www.thebooknetwork.co.uk
3. The Book Life – https://booklife.com/
4. Book Sirens – https://booksirens.com/book-reviewer-directory/nonfiction/self-help-book-reviewers?compensation_types=2&accepting_reviews_from=2
5. Book Review Directory – https://bookreviewdirectory.com/author/bookreviewdirectory/
6. http://www.theindieview.com/indie-reviewers
7. http://editing.xterraweb.com/book-reviews

Starting today, get more reviews for your book. It's never too late to start.

8

Royalties

As an author, one of the most important things you need to understand is how royalties work. After all, that's how you get paid for your book! Royalties are a percentage of the sale price that goes to the author or creator of the work. The royalty rate can vary depending on the retailer. Most eBook retailers will have different price points.

How Amazon KDP Royalties work

Amazon KDP pays royalties based on the list price of your book, minus any delivery costs. Delivery costs are calculated based on the file size of your book and the delivery method chosen. The royalty rate for each book is set by you, the author when you publish your book. Royalty rates can be anywhere from 35% to 70%, depending on the price of your book and whether you choose to enrol in KDP Select.

KDP Select is a program that allows authors to earn additional royalties by making their books available exclusively on Amazon.

Authors who enrol in KDP Select can earn royalties of up to 70% for each book sold. This includes receiving bonuses for books borrowed through the Kindle Unlimited and Prime Reading programs.

If you choose not to enrol in KDP Select, you will still earn royalties of 35% for each book sold. So, how do you know what royalty rate you're getting? Amazon has a handy **royalty calculator** that can be used to calculate the royalties you can expect to receive. If you have your own KDP account, you can easily track your royalties. If your book is hosted on a publisher's account, you will usually receive sales reports to determine the amount of money available. It's important to note that these royalty rates are only for books sold on Amazon. If your book is sold by another retailer, such as Barnes & Noble or iBooks, you will need to check their royalty rates.

Royalties are paid out 60 days after the end of the month in which the sale was made. So, if you sell a book on January 1st, you won't receive your royalties until March 1st. If you have any questions about Amazon KDP Royalties, please visit their Help Center or contact their customer service. Now that you know how Amazon KDP royalties work, you can make an informed decision about whether or not to enrol in the program.

Invoicing from bookstores

If you use a distributor, the invoicing usually happens through a publisher. Each distributor has different ways of doing business, and it is worth checking with your publisher about the terms for the book distribution, which can vary from 40 to 60 per cent of the book price. Most bookstores also charge percentage royalties; it is worth checking each consignment agreement properly and familiarising yourself with the terms of the agreement.

9

Intellectual Property and Copyright Law

I ntellectual property is a work or idea that is created by someone. This could be a book, a painting, a song, or even a design. Copyright is a form of intellectual property protection that gives authors and creators the exclusive right to reproduce, distribute, perform, display, or license their work.

Copyright law is in place to encourage creativity and prevent others from unfairly profiting from someone else's hard work. When you create something original, you automatically get copyright protection. However, registering your copyright can give you additional legal protection if you ever need to take someone to court for infringing on your work.

If you're looking to publish your work, it's important to understand both copyright and intellectual property law. Intellectual property is a broader category that includes copyright, but also extends to trademark and patent law. While copyright law covers creative works like books, music, and art, trademark law protects logos and brands, and patent law covers inventions.

So if you've created something new and unique, you'll want to file for a patent to prevent others from making, using, or selling your invention without your permission.

Copyright law is important because it helps to encourage creativity by giving creators the exclusive right to control how their work is used. This incentive encourages people to create new works, which in turn benefit society as a whole. When you create something original, you automatically get copyright protection. However, registering your copyright can give you additional legal protection in case you need to take someone to court for infringing on your work. You can always seek help from qualified professionals who will explain in more detail how to protect your work.

10

Key Relationships to Master

I n the publishing industry, there are a variety of relationships that need to be mastered to be successful. These relationships include editors, printers, PR, publishers, and bookstores. Each relationship has its own set of challenges and rewards. One of the most important relationships in publishing is between an editor and an author. A good editor can make or break a book. They work with the author to shape the book so that it is appealing to readers. Without a good editor, a book may never find its audience.

The author-publisher relationship is a symbiotic one. The author writes a work for publication, and the publisher accepts the work for publication. The dramatic difference between an unpublished manuscript and a published work is what makes this relationship possible. The former is rough and unprofessional, while the latter is polished and professional. This is because the publisher edits the manuscript to make it more effective in communicating ideas to readers.

Relationships with bookstores are crucial for authors and publishers alike. You need to be able to get your books into as many stores as possible so readers can purchase them. If a bookstore isn't interested in stocking a publisher's books, it can be very difficult for them to reach new readers, and in turn, sales can take a dip.

Another vital relationship is with a printer. A printer needs to be able to produce high-quality books promptly. If a printer is constantly delaying orders or producing subpar books, a publisher will soon find another printer. PR is also important for publishers. They need to be able to get the word out about their books and generate excitement. If a publisher doesn't have a good PR team, their books may never reach a wide audience.

Public relations

As an author, one of the best ways to build your brand and reach new readers is through public relations. By definition, public relations is the strategic process of managing the spread of information between an individual or an organization and the public. In other words, it's all about getting your name and your work out there in the world. There are a number of different ways to do public relations, but some of the most effective methods for authors include things like media relations, content marketing, and event planning. If you're looking to boost your career as an author, public relations is a great place to start.

Authors must be proactive in managing their public image and relationships with the media. Here are some tips on how to do public relations for authors:

1. Make a list of your goals. Before you start reaching out to reporters and bloggers, take a step back and think about what you want to achieve with your public relations efforts. What are your goals? Do you want to sell more books? Increase your speaking engagements. Get media coverage at specific outlets? Once you have a good understanding of your goals, you can start to develop a strategy for achieving them.

2. Research the media. Once you know your goals, you need to start doing some research. What reporters and bloggers cover your topic? What outlets are most likely to be interested in your book?

Allow me to share with you a lesson I learned the hard way: the importance of finding a good team of publishing professionals to help you produce your book.

When I first wrote my short story, "When Love Strikes," I was really excited to get it into the hands of readers and didn't do much research into the service provider I chose to help me publish it, nor did I have the knowledge about marketing and sales. Big mistake. The book went out into the world with grave grammatical errors, and it wasn't edited to publishing standards. I was livid, and I told the service provider that I would take matters into my own hands and publish it myself since they refused to make corrections, citing the amount I had paid them at the time.

So I did DIY and I learned a lot in the process.

Now, I've developed a good rapport with editors, designers, web developers, printers, people in the media, and other publishing professionals because I've learned that producing a book takes a community. It's not one person's job.

It is important to connect with purposeful service providers who can help you get your book into the hands of the right people. Don't make the same mistakes I did.

11

Marketing and Promotions

U sing different marketing techniques can help speed up the process of building an audience. Following relevant people in your niche via social media will give you content ideas and tips on how to promote yourself effectively. Utilise all channels available to you when promoting your work—write blog posts, publish podcasts, share videos, and upload posts into Facebook groups targeted at specific audiences. Building an engaged base of followers takes time, but is well worth the effort given the positive results it produces in the end!

The digitisation of books has been a growing trend in recent years, and it is not showing any signs of slowing down. This is largely due to the convenience and accessibility that digital books offer. In addition, the COVID pandemic has further accelerated this trend as people look for ways to access content remotely.

What can authors do about it? There are several things authors can do to ensure they are keeping up with this trend. First and foremost, they need to be aware of the trend and the potential implications for their business. Secondly, they need to consider how they can make their content more accessible in digital form. This may involve digitising existing content or creating new digital content from scratch. Finally, authors need to stay up-to-date with the latest developments in digital book technology so that they can take advantage of new opportunities as they arise.

There are several different ways to digitise books, so it is important to choose the right method for your needs. One popular option is to use an ebook converter, which can quickly and easily convert your book into digital format. Another option is to use a service like Amazon Kindle Direct Publishing, which allows you to publish your book electronically on the Kindle platform. Whichever route you decide to go down, be sure to consider the benefits of beta readers.

Talking about your book before it's written

You might be wondering when the best time is to start marketing your book. Before you even begin writing, this is the answer. That's right—talking about your book before it's even written can help you get published.

Here's how:

1. Talking about your book can generate interest and excitement among potential readers. This could help you get a publishing deal, as publishers are always on the lookout

for books that will make the bestseller's list.

2. Talking about your book could also help you refine your ideas and plot. As you discuss your book with others, you may get feedback and suggestions that will improve the final product.

3. Finally, talking about your book gives you a chance to practice your pitch. When you're ready to query agents or publishers, you'll already have a well-rehearsed elevator pitch.

So don't be afraid to start talking about your book today; it could be the key to getting it published tomorrow.

Your Marketing Plan

In order to structure a marketing plan for your book, consider the following 8Ps of your book journey:

1. Product: what is the title of your book?
2. Price: how much will it cost?
3. Place: where will you be selling the book?
4. Promotion: how will you sell it?
5. People: who is the perfect buyer for your book?
6. Process: what processes will you use?
7. Personalization: how can you tailor your messaging to your ideal customer?
8. Physical evidence: what design will be used to make the book more appealing?

SEO/Marketing Techniques

If you're an author with a website, SEO is essential to helping people find your work online. Here are some tips on how to master SEO like a pro:

1. Use relevant keywords throughout your website, in the titles and body of text.
2. Make sure your website is well-designed and easy to navigate; this will help search engines index your site correctly.
3. Use social media to promote your work; this will help create backlinks to your site, which is good for SEO.
4. Regularly update your website with new content; this will keep people coming back, and also help you rank higher in search results.

Following these tips can help ensure that your website is optimised for SEO and that you're getting the most out of your online presence.

Reader Magnets and Email Lists

A reader magnet is anything that you can give away to your readers in exchange for them doing something you want them to do. This can be signing up for your mailing list, which will attract more readers and have them follow you as you offer them ebooks, discount coupons, course discounts, audio files, and so forth.

A reader magnet attracts and connects. Imagine being offered an e-book, book chapters, or an interesting audio file just for signing up for an author's mailing list. This actually brings in:

1. Motivation for your readers – once offered something, even a discount, a reader is motivated to sign up for your mailing list.
2. It helps sell a lot of books in a short period of time. For instance, if one is offered a discount they are likely to pay for or buy the book increasing their profits, number of customers and a large variety of people following them.
3. It attracts readers through many channels through a blog, advertising, or social media.

A mailing list allows an author to email their readers every time they have a new release. You may not start off with a lot of people on your mailing list, but as you grow and progress in your author journey, your list will also grow. A mailing list helps with:

1. Communicating directly with the audience is more effective than that social media. Also having a mailing list can help if, in the future, you lose access to your social media platforms...you will recover your audience because you will have the permission of people to communicate with them.
2. Building a relationship with potential customers – most people are likely to buy through their email from someone they know.

12

Social Media Influence

The use of social media to promote books, publications, and authors has become a trend that is important for publishers to implement. Social media engages readers in ways that many traditional avenues of marketing cannot. Creating an effective social media marketing strategy for your publications is the first step, and this should be monitored regularly. It is important that publishers leverage the importance of using social media.

To start, the author should communicate the core message to their readers in their marketing campaign. They should ask themselves the questions;

1. What are the consumer needs?
2. How relevant and different is the content that I produce,
3. Does the content match the audience's needs?

When creating a social media campaign, the author should

think about how they can trend and grab the reader's attention. Hashtags are commonly used to track trends. Social media platforms like Twitter can make a hashtag trend, while on Instagram, one can search for a hashtag and find the author's work. Through a hashtag, an author is visible, and their search engine optimisation increases. Hashtags help mark keywords and let other people create a trend around the hashtag. A hashtag should be well thought out and creative. An author should have unique knowledge of their online community to help with the marketing campaign.

The marketing campaign may not be successful if there is a sudden drop after an event or publication. As an author, you might think about a countdown or a feature of the book topics. A behind-the-scenes look can help with preparation before a release. A successful social media marketing strategy delves deep into the upcoming book before it is even launched. If planned in advance, there can even be requests from the intended audience on what they desire. Social media offerings around a publication may reduce the perceived risk for the potential consumer because they offer the opportunity to engage with the content prior to purchasing it and get a first impression as to whether the publication will meet expectations.

The type of content matters as well. To be interesting, the content must be diverse. A writer can utilise videos as well as words, but they must be no longer than 30 seconds. Polls and Q&As can also be utilised on websites like Twitter, which is useful for answering sporadic text inquiries, and Instagram Live, which is useful for focused Q&A sessions. The most well-liked images, together with live streaming, reels, and links to landing pages, can all be utilised. Note that a landing page sends social media followers to a website where they can find out more or make purchases. For example, if the author has their book uploaded on Amazon, they can share a link to the Amazon site. The content that a publisher shares on their page should follow a consistent approach. This can be accompanied by post formatting style, a set time schedule, brand voice and identity, as well as content type consistency.

The preference for social media sites varies. Each social network has different content requirements, hosts different audiences, and provides unique promotional opportunities. The trick again is to understand your audience and customer personas. Depending on the type of information that is to be distributed and the type of readers a publisher has, certain social networks might not work for them. It is important that a publisher be aware of who their audience is. It becomes apparent from the research that Facebook seems to be the most popular for businesses.

Social Media Platforms

Creating a Facebook page can easily bring individuals with common interests together. To keep a page active, one may post cover reveals, start discussions around the publication, and actively share and post stories. There may be no need to be present on TikTok or Snapchat if the audience is mature or businesspeople. Instagram, from research, has been discovered to have the majority of users who are between the ages of 18 and 29, followed by 30-49. Instagram is most effective for visual content, such as a book cover. The people who use this platform are mostly there to discover, entertain themselves and feel inspired.

Twitter is good for connecting with people outside of your followers as finding an audience for your content can trend by using hashtags, and retweeting. One may conclude that if pictures are more your thing, prioritize Instagram. If you're witty, Twitter might be the best option. If your audience is a bit mature, Facebook has to be the best. The specifics of strategy vary for each publisher, and the only way to identify which social media strategy will work best for you is to step back and think carefully about your strengths, audience, and goals.

Social media offers sponsored posts or paid-for advertising. Marketing can be controlled by paying. Companies that sponsor posts decide what to say and where that advertising will appear. In most instances, sponsored posts are best used when one is new to social media and is trying to get a following as fast as possible. Sponsored posts can be used regularly to keep publishers and authors boosted in their posts. The focus of sponsored posts is on achieving a solid return on investment at a faster rate within the designated time frame. Most social media platforms use cost-per-click (CPC) structures for advertising, which means you only pay if people click on your ad. There are also cost-per-thousand impressions, in which you pay for people to see your ad, whether they interact with it or not.

Being on social media requires you to use it effectively. Once you've built your social media following, it is important to take time to hear customers' feedback on your work. Publishers should network with each other, as it is not all competition.

Social media is a great way to connect with other authors. You can share their content with your followers and promote the people you care about.

Social media may not be too focused on selling, but remember it is "social!" The drive should be to foster a connection. Often authors focus only on promotion, asking everyone to buy their book and never interacting on a human level. If this is done well and helps build up platforms and relationships on Twitter, Facebook, and Instagram, the sales will come later. In this sense, results are a product of building confidence with your audience over time. In the world of social media, marketing amounts to making friends.

13

Monetising your book idea

Different ways to monetise your books:

Audiobooks

Turning your books into audio format is one of the most important tools for digitisation. Audiobooks provide an easy way to turn paperbacks into audio. They're essential for people who want to keep up with the latest books. Audiobooks also have several benefits, including the ability to help people learn new languages and improve their reading comprehension. Audiobooks are an essential part of the modern world, and they're only going to become more important in the future.

Podcasts

Podcasts are fun, engaging, and entertaining ways of obtaining information, and more and more authors are turning to podcasts to keep their audiences tuned in.

Ebooks

Selling ebooks is a great way to reach more readers and earn more revenue. But how do you actually go about selling ebooks? First, you'll need to choose a platform to sell your ebooks on. There are a number of different ebook platforms out there, so it's important to choose one that will reach your target readership. Once you've chosen a platform, you'll need to format your ebook and create an attractive cover. Then, you can start marketing your ebook and driving sales. With a little effort, you can easily start selling ebooks and reaching a wider audience for your work.

Hardcover format

The hardcover format appeals to books that require this adaptable finish and is especially useful for some book kinds, such as those that readers desire to keep as keepsakes and reference materials. Yearbooks, children's books, and art books are popular examples of books that people prefer to showcase on coffee tables. Professionally printed volumes like textbooks for the fields of medicine, law, architecture, or engineering are perfect candidates for this binding finish. This binding choice is suitable for self-published publications as well because it gives the item a distinctive and personalised finish that gives it an air of quality, class, and legitimacy.

Paperback format

The paperback format is the most common and widely sold in print. Most authors prefer to print copies of their books and sell them to recover publishing costs. This is independent of platforms such as Amazon. Having printed copies on hand is also useful if you need to distribute your book to bookstores, either through a publisher or a book distributor.

Turning your book into a film

If you are into fiction, you have no doubt seen books that have been turned into series and movies. The rise of film adaptations means that many books have the potential to be turned into films. Although it can be a costly endeavour, the benefits outweigh the risks because you can pitch your story ideas to directors and film producers, who in turn can pay for your contribution.

Book Distribution

With print-on-demand printing, a single copy of your book will be produced and dispatched to the buyer as soon as an order is received and payment is received. The disadvantage of only printing books when they are requested is that you are likely not going to see your books on brick-and-mortar retail shelves across the country (or even regionally). The largest US book wholesaler and distributor is Ingram, which operates IngramSpark. Amazon KDP has no upfront costs or charges; however, self-publishing authors will charge you to get your book formatted correctly to KDP standards. Other book distributors include book distributors, wholesalers, and bookstores such as Waterstones and WHSmith.

14

How to stay relevant after publishing your book

When you're marketing your book, it's important to be creative and think outside the box. There are several ways to get your book noticed, and it's up to you to find the ones that work best for you and your book. Be sure to be active on social media, do book launches, appear on podcasts and radio interviews, and have a mailing list. You can also make your books available in different formats to increase sales. By being creative and thinking outside the box, you'll be sure to stay relevant after publishing your book. So you've put in the work, struggled with writing, and now your "baby" is in your hands. Now what? The **key** to staying relevant is to:

Throw a Book Launch

It's time to celebrate! You've put in the work; now throw a book launch to celebrate your hard work. This can be an excellent opportunity to invite renowned guests who can help market your book further. Attending other book launches and reading events also helps spread the message about your book. Hosting book events such as book clubs can attract new readers and help you with sales.

Leverage your online presence for success

Being present on social media is essential for developing your author brand. Connect with your followers and engage with them, often hosting giveaways or inviting guests on your platform to discuss trending topics, whether related to your book or current affairs. You can find ways to stand out from the crowd. This can be done in a variety of ways, from choosing a specific niche or market group (i.e., best books for pre-teens) to determining whether there is a large enough market for the book through quick and easy research.

Create a blog

If you're a writer, starting a blog is a great way to promote your work and build an audience for your book. A lot of people use and rely on the internet daily, and blogging has become a very profitable business. For sustainability, specialising in one area of interest is important. Book blogs are trendy among readers and writers who need exposure for their books. A blog can help you connect with readers and give them a taste of your writing style. It can also be a great platform for sharing book excerpts, conducting interviews, and providing behind-the-scenes information about your writing process. Of course, starting a blog takes time and effort, but it's well worth it if you're serious about promoting your work. A blog can help you build an audience for your book, connect with other writers, and share your thoughts and ideas with the world.

Grow an email list

Your readers want to hear from you, and this is one of the ways to do it. Carry scannable QR codes with an effective Call To Action (CTA). An effective CTA could include offering a free ebook in exchange for contact details or driving your book sales.

Start a podcast

If your book has 10 chapters, you are potentially looking at 20 episodes of podcasting. You can invite other experts to talk about certain topics that you have highlighted in your book. You can also make money while doing this by way of advertising and getting other brands interested in your work.

Turn your book into an audio format

Producing audiobooks is a fantastic way for authors to reach a new audience, promote inspiration, and enhance new skills. Not only is spoken word time-saving, but it is also helpful so you can focus on other tasks. **Readers report that listening to audiobooks helps them remember information better than reading.** It improves memory and has the ability to boost our moods and disrupt negative thinking patterns, making it a terrific way to reduce stress and help with mental stimulation. In the transition from paperback to audiobooks, authors can play an active role in society by including disadvantaged or disabled members of society, specifically the blind.

Turn your book into a film

Adapting a film based on a book allows the author to tap into an audience they would otherwise not have reached through their book. The majority of people nowadays prefer to watch films based on books rather than read the book itself. The question then becomes, "How can I, as an author, best get more people to know my story?" Create a movie based on your book! A thousand-page book can be summed up into a one-hour, thirty-minute film, or a series, which is the preferred entertainment for the majority. Book genres that seem to be popular in this regard are fiction, autobiographies, and science fiction.

The use of subtitles in the film helps eliminate language barriers, and some viewers go on to learn new languages as a result of watching the film. Film adaptations can also be said to be solving the problem of illiteracy in various communities that either do not prioritise reading or are unable to afford to purchase books for entertainment purposes. Adapting a book into a film brings the author's imagination into reality, although not quite as close as the one the author might have had.

Collect book reviews

Book reviews are a great way to gain credibility with your readers. You need readers for your book to sell. Word of mouth from readers can be a powerful tool in getting your book picked up and sales moving quickly. Refer to the Reviews chapter to find out more about book reviews.

I wish you the best of luck with your book project!

About the Author

Rudo Muchoko, as a creative, publisher, and author, has become a fervent supporter of publishing works. She writes, edits, and publishes books, magazines, and audiobooks with the aim to lead and mentor authors using the suggestions in her book *Awakening the Power of Self Publishing: the ultimate Guide.*

You can connect with me on:

🌐 https://www.rmpbookcafe.com

📘 https://www.facebook.com/RMPublishers

🔗 https://www.thebooknetwork.co.uk/the-blog

🔗 https://www.brainzmagazine.com/executive-contributor/Rudo-Muchoko

🔗 https://www.instagram.com/rwashe_m

Subscribe to my newsletter:

✉️ https://rm-pa.org

Printed by Amazon Italia Logistica S.r.l.
Torrazza Piemonte (TO), Italy

43656950R00047